For Rosa and Trudi – T.M.

For Sian and Laura

and special thanks for the Goldy magic – G.P-R.

ISBN 0-439-67860-9

First published in Great Britain in 2003 by Orchard Books London. Text copyright © 2003 by Tony Mitton. Illustrations copyright © 2003 by Guy Parker-Rees. All rights reserved. Published by Orchard Books, an imprint of Scholastic Inc. ORCHARD BOOKS and design are registered trademarks of Watts Publishing Group, Ltd., used under license. SCHOLASTIC and associated logos are trademarks and/or registered trademarks of Scholastic Inc.

12 11 10 9 8 7 6 5 4 3 2 1   4 5 6 7 8 9/0

Printed in the U.S.A.   40

First Scholastic paperback printing, October 2004

Spooky Hour

By Tony Mitton

Illustrated by Guy Parker-Rees

SCHOLASTIC INC.

New York   Toronto   London   Auckland   Sydney
Mexico City   New Delhi   Hong Kong   Buenos Aires

BONG! goes the bell in the rickety tower,
Twelve times...that means it's Spooky Hour.

Listen! Hush! Oooh, what's that sound?
The midnight spooks are coming 'round.

Then off they zoom on broomsticks, "Wheeeeee!"

Out of the darkness, what's this here?

Ten funny, floaty ghosts appear,

Nine skeletons dance by, clickety clack.
Their snapping teeth go snickety snack.

At the edge of the trees, tu-whit tu-whoo,
Eight spooky owls hoot, "We'll come, too."

Leaping high
and
creeping low,

Seven scary cats with eyes that glow!

From deep in the woods comes a rumbling sound,

As **SIX** trolls tromp the **grumbling** ground.

And what's that scuttling?

Better be wary...

Five
big
spiders,
fat
and
hairy.

Shadows leap as your heart beats quicker.
Through the trees comes a splutter-and-flicker.

Four wizards, holding lanterns bright,
Go by in dancing candlelight.

Beside the gate to the castle yard,
Three suits of armor stand on guard.

A noise comes swirling down the stair.

Let's go on up. Oh, do we dare?

"Cackle cackle...tee-hee-hee..."

I wonder who that is?

Let's see...

...rise!"

two big grins,

Are Mitch and Titch,

the witchy twins.

And what's this here?

Oh me, oh my!

It's...

The spooks all cry out, "Yum! Yum! Yum!"
And they eat up every single crumb.

Then Mitch says, "Come on, everyone. Let's have some scary party fun!"

They hide away
in funny places,
Then pop out:

BOO!

with spooky faces.

They leap and swirl,
they howl and shriek,
As they play at screechy
hide-and-seek.

But even spooks can have enough,
And in the end, they're out of puff.

As the morning sun begins to rise,
They start to yawn and rub their eyes.

They stretch,
and scratch
their sleepy heads...

Then home they go to snuggly beds.